I Went Walking

WRITTEN BY

Sue Williams

ILLUSTRATED BY

Julie Vivas

Voyager Books • Harcourt, Inc.

San Diego   New York   London

Manufactured in China

I went walking.

What did you see?

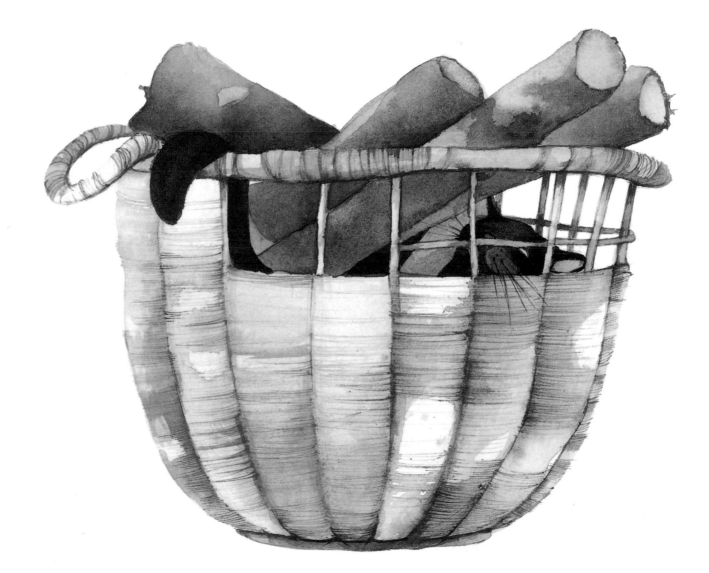

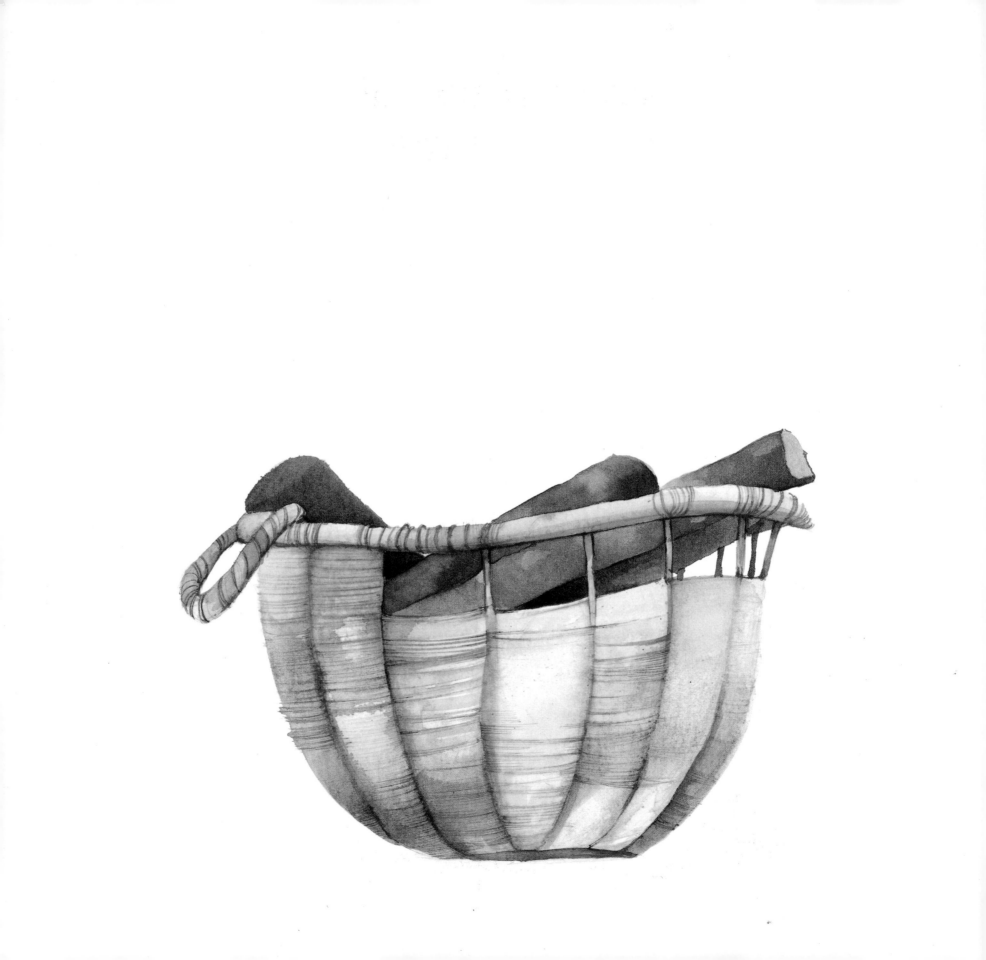

I saw a black cat
Looking at me.

I went walking.

What did you see?

I saw a brown horse
Looking at me.

I went walking.

What did you see?

I saw a red cow
Looking at me.

I went walking.

What did you see?

I saw a green duck
Looking at me.

I went walking.

What did you see?

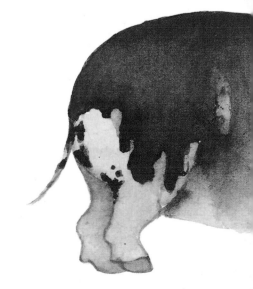

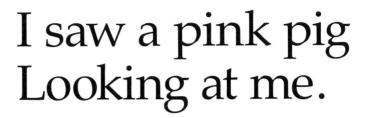

I saw a pink pig
Looking at me.

I went walking.

What did you see?

I saw a yellow dog
Looking at me.

I went walking.

What did you see?

I saw a lot of animals
Following me!

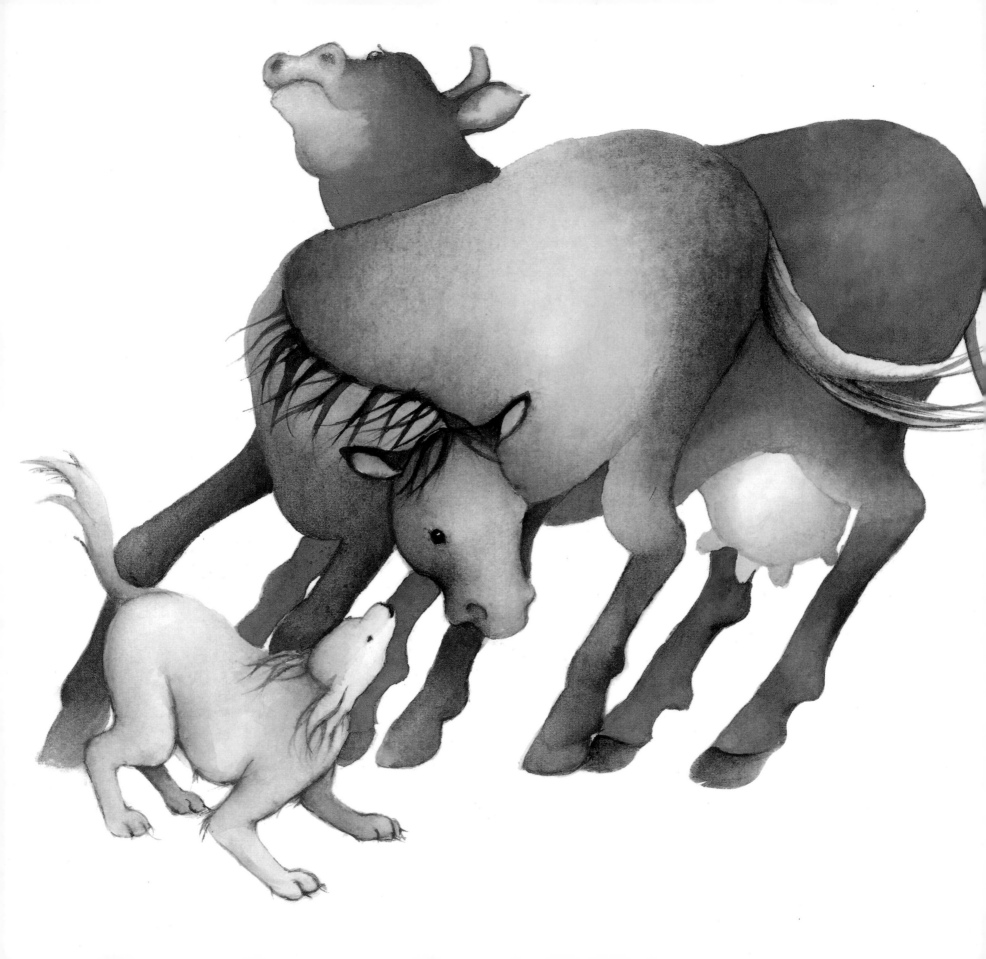

Voyager Books is a registered trademark of Harcourt, Inc.

First published 1989 by Omnibus Books
First U.S. edition 1990

The Library of Congress has cataloged the hardcover edition as follows:
Williams, Sue.
I went walking / written by Sue Williams; illustrated by Julie Vivas.
p. cm.
Summary: During the course of a walk, a young boy identifies
animals of different colors.
[1. Walking—Fiction. 2. Color—Fiction. 3. Animals—Fiction.
4. Stories in rhyme.] I. Vivas, Julie, 1947– ill. II. Title.
PZ8.3.M1569Iaw   1990   [E]—dc20   89-78475
ISBN 0-15-200471-8
ISBN 0-15-238011-6 pb
ISBN 0-15-200771-7 board book
ISBN 0-15-238010-8 oversize pb

P R T V X W U S Q O

Manufactured in China